DAJAH AND THE BEAST

BY DAJAH NEVAEH

To order additional copies of this book, contact:
Xlibris
844-714-8691
www.Xlibris.com
Orders@Xlibris.com

ISBN: Softcover   978-1-6698-6004-4
        EBook   978-1-6698-6005-1

Print information available on the last page

Rev. date: 12/29/2022

Dajah is a kindergarten student at Francis Marion Elementary School. Dajah is on the honor roll.

She loves reading, math and playing songs on her keyboard.

Dajah was inspired to write this book when she got with the corona virus.

SPECIAL THANKS

To my Lord above. My mother, Ms. Virginie F. Nemo
My grandparents, Francita Nemo
and Charles E. McCleeney
My aunts, Annie (Billie) Lucky and Carrie Nemo,
my wonderful God mother Kay Wand Skipper
And Please Please ...

God Bless my Daddy Daniel Bailey

Special Thanks to "DSLH"

I love you all!!

Dajah Nemo

Once upon a time, a little girl named Dajah love to have fun and play with her toys. She likes to play outdoors riding her bike, swinging on her swing and jumping on her trampoline.

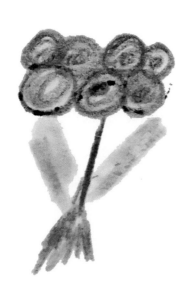

One day, she woke up very sick. She was coughing and had a high fever. Dajah's mother, Nana and Godmother carried her to the doctor.

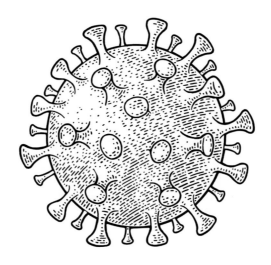

The Doctor said she had covid-19, the BEAST

I knew I was going to get better because
I was going to beat that BEAST

I had to take lots of medicines, rest and eat chicken noodle soup.

I had to wear a mask on my face. I was sad.

I could not go outside and play. I had to stay in my room for fourteen days. I was crying. I remember what my Nana said, "Dajah, you can do all things through CHRIST, who strengthen you." I decided to fight that Corona Beast. I began to pray.

Every day, I would pray, wash my hands singing
the ABC song, wear my mask and keep
my playroom and toys wash.

In a few days I will start to feel better. I won!!
I won!! I beat that BEAST, the Coronavirus.

My advice to everyone is listen to your doctor,
wash your hands. Wear your mask.

If you are sick please stay home
and don't forget to pray.
That's how I beat that BEAST, COVID 19

THE END

THE   BEAST

DAIAH

Dajah is a kindergarten student at Francis Marion Elementary School. Dajah is on the honor roll.

She loves reading, math and playing songs on her keyboard.

Dajah was inspired to write this book when she got with the corona virus.

Printed in the United States
by Baker & Taylor Publisher Services